EZRA DAWN

The Warden's Easter Trap
Ezra Dawn

Cover art created by JeB Designs
jebdesigns@outlook.com

The Surgeon's Instant Family © 2019 Ezra Dawn
eBook ISBN: 978100575154
ISBN-13: 9798721464799

Table of Contents

Character Name Pronunciation

Prologue

Chapter One

Chapter Two

Chapter Three

Chapter Four

Chapter Five

Chapter Six

Chapter Seven

Chapter Eight

Chapter Nine

Epilogue

Playlists

Acknowledgements

About the Author

Other Books by Ezra

CHARACTER NAME Pronunciation

Cotton Daniels (Cot-ton, Dan-yells)

Everett Michaelis (Ever-ett, Me-kay-lis)

ABOUT THE

(The Warden's Easter Trap is a short story and a complete standalone with the instalove of fated mates.)

Cotton Daniels is a Flemish Giant Rabbit shifter on the run from his herd and has been labeled a rogue. He's been travelling for weeks trying to put as much distance between him and his hometown as possible. On his way to find a council member to plead his case, he hops right into a trap.

Game Warden Everett Michaelis is a black bear shifter who loves his job. He's just wrapped up a poaching case that got a little too close to home when he gets a call from a fellow sleuth member whose children are screaming about the easter bunny dying. Everett arrives on scene half-expecting to have to put the rabbit out of its misery but instead he gets the surprise of his life.

Can Everett save Cotton from his injuries and his past or will the things Cotton is running from keep them apart?

(**Warning:** *Contains graphic sexual content and explicit language. Not recommended for those under the age of 18.*)

Trigger Warning

This book contains a brief description of attempted
rape that may be a trigger for some.

PROLOGUE

One month ago...

I'm walking through the woods on my way to the lake for a swim when I'm suddenly tackled from the side. I hit the ground hard, and the breath leaves my lungs from the impact. My attacker straddles my hips and leers down at me. "Finally caught you alone."

Damn it...he's the one person I'd hoped to avoid. Peter the herd alpha's son has been trying to get in my pants for weeks and has refused to take no for an answer. "Get off me, Peter."

Peter laughs evilly, "Oh, I'll get off alright. You're going to give me what I want, you little tease."

My blood runs cold as the meaning of his words register. "I told you I wasn't interested. Get off me now or I'll scream."

"I don't care what you said. I want you and I aim to have you. Go ahead and scream no one will hear you."

My fight or flight instincts kick in and I try to get out from under him. He's bigger than me and heavier so I don't succeed in bucking him off. Calling on my self-defense training, I gouge his eyes, punch him in the nose, and am about to punch him in the throat but he dodges by smacking my arm away. Peter growls and slaps me across the face. "Stop struggling, damnit."

When he reaches for my swim trunks and starts to pull them down, I know I've got to do something to get away since nothing else is working. Looking around, I spot a big rock to my right. Grabbing it, I club Peter over the head with it as hard as I can. Peter slumps to the side and I squirm away from him. Jumping to my feet, I right my shorts then take off running. Fifteen minutes later, before I reach my cabin, my best friend steps into my path with a backpack slung over his shoulder. Skidding to a stop, I ask, "Going somewhere, Kee?"

Keenan shakes his head. "No, but you are. Peter called the alpha and said you attacked him. The alpha is out for blood. If you return now, he'll have you killed on sight. I know you wouldn't attack Peter without a good reason so I'm going to make sure you get away from here."

He hands me the backpack and says, "I packed you some clothes, money, and food. I'm going to pack up everything in your cabin and put it in storage. I'd recommend stopping at a bank on your way and withdrawing everything you have then cut up your credit cards because they'll surely try to track you through those transactions. When you settle somewhere new, send me an email or a letter under an assumed name with your address and I'll have your things shipped to you. Give me your phone and get out of here."

It hurts knowing I have to leave my home because of an asshole but Keenan's right. If I want to live, I have to leave. Maybe when I get settled somewhere new, I can contact the shifter council and explain my side of things. I hand Keenan my phone, take the backpack, and hug him tight. "I'm going to miss you my friend."

"I'll miss you too. Now go before they find you."

Nodding, I put the backpack over my shoulders and take off running.

CHAPTER ONE

Present Day...

I've been on the run for a month. By some miracle, I managed to escape the enforcers' clutches and get to town. After withdrawing every penny from my bank accounts, I bought a cheap used car and paid extra for the salesman to put a fake name on the paperwork and look the other way on keeping an I.D. on file. Once I had the car, I headed west choosing to sleep in the car instead of getting hotels so my money would go as far as possible. I'm a video game programmer so I can work from anywhere but after being off the radar for a month I probably won't have a job to go back to. Which is fine, I guess. I can always find another job with a different company. If I'm not in jail that is. I did love my job though. I've always had a knack for computers and enjoy taking them apart and putting them back together.

When I took a programming class in college, I found my calling and instead of getting my degree in computer science, I focused on programming and game design. For my senior year, I developed a game app that I sold to the company I ended up working for. It made me millions, but I had the common sense to put that money in a bank account at a bank in New York near the game company's headquarters under an alias.

My hometown is small, and herd run, and I know if I'd put the money I made off the game app into my account, the entire herd would know how much I'm worth. Once that knowledge got out, people like Peter and the alpha would try to con me out of my money somehow. Whether it was in herd tithes or having one of the members try and get me to bond with them, so they'd automatically have half. Hell, I wouldn't have been surprised if they'd gone so far as to beat the crap out of me until I agreed to turn it over. In fact, in order to avoid that kind of situation, I only had a small portion of my paycheck deposited into my account at the town bank. The rest went into the other account with my millions in it.

After I hit the road, I made it as far as Washington that first day before my car crapped out. Knowing I didn't want to be stuck for days or weeks getting it fixed by a mechanic I decided to continue my journey on foot. After selling the car to a junkyard for scrap, I went to a sporting goods store where I bought the supplies I'd need for camping, a bow and arrows for hunting, a collapsible fishing pole for fishing, clothes appropriate for hiking, and a larger backpack to store everything including all my cash, so I could stick to the forest to cross the border into Canada.

I've heard the wolf representative for the shifter council is based in Alaska so that's where I'm heading. I should be going to the rabbit representative but since rabbits can't scent lies like wolves can, I'm hoping the wolf representative will let me plead my case instead of tossing me in jail and leaving me there until a trial can be held. I have no doubts that the alpha of my herd has named me a rogue and pressed charges for the attack on his son. I'm sure Peter didn't tell his father why I attacked him because he'd never own up to his actions.

The man is an entitled prick who thinks he's the gods' gift to everyone. He doesn't believe it when someone says they're not interested in him. Instead, he sees it as them playing hard to get. I'm sure I'm not the only one he's assaulted but since no one has reported him, he keeps getting away with it. *If my plan works, he won't get away with it this time.*

For weeks now, I've hiked as far as I could during the day before setting up camp only to tear it down and be on my way the next day. My father was in the military and taught his kids everything he knew about how to survive in the wilderness including how to cure the meat from the game we hunted so it would last a few days without spoiling. He'd test us on what we learned by taking each of us into different parts of the woods during every season so we couldn't help each other then left us to fend for ourselves.

The first few times he was nearby in case we struggled but once we got the hang of it, he'd leave us for an entire week instead of a couple days. That training was something I never thought I'd have to use outside of a vacation retreat capacity, but it's been a lifesaver. When it's safe to contact my family, I'll have to thank my dad for making sure I had the knowledge needed to live off the land. But first I have to get out of the mess I'm in.

I crossed into Alaska a few days ago but according to the map I printed off at an internet café, I've got another day of hiking ahead of me before I reach the town where the wolf shifter representative lives. I couldn't get his exact address off the council website so when I get to town I'll have to ask around about where to find him and pray I'm not making a mistake by showing up on his doorstep unannounced.

Once I get in town, I'll see about booking a motel room for a night so I can clean up. I've washed my clothes and bathed in rivers when I could, but it's been about a week since I last came across one and I have to be honest, I reek. I've found creeks where I refilled my canteen, but they weren't big enough or deep enough for bathing. I haven't shaved since before I left home so I'm certain I look like a scrawny lumberjack wearing a dead animal on my face. My beard and mustache are that thick and unruly.

The sun is setting so I set up camp for the night and cook up the last of the meat from the deer I killed the other day. What I don't eat tonight will be my breakfast in the morning before I continue my hike. After I've eaten, I pack what's left of the meat into the box that blocks the scent of it, so I don't attract any wildlife, then I douse the flames and head into my tent. It's a bit early to go to sleep but I'm tired and need the rest so I can get an early start. Pouring some water in my cup, I use it to brush my teeth and rinse my mouth out, then I dump the cup outside the tent before zipping the door flap shut. Stripping out of my clothes, I climb into my bedroll and close my eyes letting sleep take me.

The next morning as the sun is rising, I eat breakfast and tear down my campsite, packing everything away in my backpack. When I'm sure I've got everything, I continue on the path to town. I'm halfway into the trip when I decide to stop for lunch and to let my rabbit out for a bit. Being in nature always has my rabbit excited to be let out so I try to shift at least once a day. Grabbing a couple protein bars from my pack, I scarf them and chase them down with water from my canteen.

Needing to stash my pack where no one will find it, I climb a tree and tie it to a branch. Stripping out of my clothes, I fold them up and tuck them inside a hole at the base of the tree then initiate my shift. Shaking out my fur, I hop away from the tree to explore the woods around me. I've been at it for an hour when I spot a bunch of log cabins through the trees. Curiosity gets the best of me and I hop closer to them. I'm within two hundred feet of one of the cabins when I hear a metal click before a bear trap springs up and clamps on my back legs. White hot agony shoots through my body and I wonder if this is how I'm going to die before my world goes black.

CHAPTER TWO

I finish writing up the report on the poacher case I just closed that got a little too close to home. Some men were hunting on the land my sleuth owns and resides on. The sheer amount of bear traps they'd lain out was appalling and completely reckless. If a shifter child had gotten caught in one of them it could've spelled disaster. The sleuth enforcers have been scouring the forest in an effort to remove all the traps but with the men refusing to admit just how many traps they set there's no way to know if all of them have been found. Considering each trap adds another charge I can see why they don't want to get themselves in more trouble.

The men aren't from around here which explains why they got too close to trapping and killing shifters. Killua, named after Killua Mountain is a very small town. Most of the residents are paranormals though the majority of them are shifters. The few humans that live in this town know exactly what we are, and they keep our secret because this community is so close knit. We rarely have any crime here. For the most part it's just teenagers committing petty acts of crime.

The crime rate does climb around hunting season because we have people from other towns coming out to hunt. It also climbs around tourist season because we have people coming to stay at the Killua Mountain Resort which only opens for half the year since winters here are so harsh. As a game warden, I also have my peace officer's certification, so I have the authority to arrest anyone committing a crime if I happen to catch them in the act. I've always loved the forest thanks to my animal half and as a kid, I wanted to be a forest ranger so I could spend all my time in nature but that all changed when I was a teenager.

While out on a run I came across a couple of men poaching some deer. From a young age, every child in the sleuth was taught to stick close to the cabins during hunting season. We learned all about when hunting season would start, which animals were being hunted and which weapons were being used during those times. When I came across the poachers, I knew for a fact it wasn't hunting season, so I committed their faces and the license plate of their truck to memory before I raced home and reported them to the game warden.

When the men were caught, I was proud of myself for helping bring them to justice and the rest is history. Instead of going into the forest service when I turned eighteen, I entered the academy to become a game warden. I've been working the job ever since. The fact that I don't have to remake my identity and move away for a while because the townsfolk are in the know about my lack of aging is an added bonus. I'm happy with my life but I have to admit, I'm also lonely. Some of my friends have found their mates and settled down already and it makes me long for a mate of my own to share my life with.

Coming home to an empty house isn't fun and it's not like my fish can talk back so I've got no one to talk about my day with. My friends don't count because I don't share an intimate connection with any of them. If I did, their mates would string me up by my toes and beat me like a pinata for trying to poach their men. Not that I'd ever do such a thing. I don't have a death wish.

After I've printed my report, I tuck it into the case file and put it away before I finish eating my lunch. Instead of staying on patrol, I came back to the office to get the report done, so I wouldn't have to do it tonight after my shift is over. As I'm taking my last bite of sandwich, my phone rings. Unclipping it from the case on my belt, I answer. "Hello?"

"Everett, this is Clara, we've got a situation." I hear children screaming and crying in the background about the easter bunny dying as Clara explains, "There's a rabbit caught in a bear trap behind my house. You'd better get here quick."

Standing, I say, "I'll be there in a few minutes," and end the call. I forgot about today being easter. The kids were probably looking for eggs when they found the rabbit. *What a nightmare.* Rushing out of the office, I climb into my truck and start it up, turning on the flashing lights, I pull out of the lot and race to sleuth lands. Clara and her family live in a cabin ten houses from mine. The fact that the enforcers missed a trap so close to her home is worrisome. I'll have to talk to the alpha about getting some metal detectors to scan for the traps to make sure more didn't get missed. We don't need anyone else getting hurt.

Parking my truck in front of Clara's house, I circle around to the back of the cabin where she's standing on her porch hugging her distraught children. "Where's the rabbit?"

Clara points to the woods directly behind the house and I head that way. The scent of blood hits my nose and I have to fight my bear from coming out. *The rabbit is my mate.* Knowing he's hurt has my bear wanting to rip someone to shreds but I can't do that. Helping my injured mate comes first. When I find the rabbit, a whimper of anguish escapes. Seeing his grey fur matted with blood and his left hind leg mangled by the trap hurts my heart. Thank gods he's a shifter and way larger than the average rabbit otherwise he'd have lost that leg completely. *If I get my hands on the assholes who set these traps when no one is around, I'll kill them and make it look like an accident.*

Pulling my uniform shirt from where it's tucked in my pants, I unbutton it and tear a long strip from the bottom of my undershirt. Kneeling on the ground, I tie the strip of fabric around his leg and tie it tight enough to hopefully slow or stop the bleeding. He's lost enough blood as it is, if he loses anymore, I could lose him. *I hope fate wouldn't be so cruel as to give me my mate only to take him away from me.* The poor thing has passed out either from the pain or the blood loss, maybe both. Even though I know he can't hear me, I stroke his fur and say, "This is going to hurt like a motherfucker beautiful. I hate to cause you anymore pain but I need to get you out of here." Gripping the trap, I pull it apart and free his leg.

Hearing him screech, I apologize profusely, feeling tears prick my eyes. "Sorry, sorry, I know it hurts." Ripping a wider strip from my undershirt, I wrap it around his leg as carefully as I can then I carefully pick him up. Standing, I jog back through the woods taking care not to jostle him too much. Skirting Clara's cabin, I head to my truck. Depositing the rabbit on a blanket I have in the backseat I get behind the wheel and put it in gear, thankful that I left it running. Turning the truck around, I race back to town, praying the rabbit doesn't die before I get him to the doctor.

Screeching to a stop in front of the clinic, I hop out and gently grab my charge from the backseat hating the little whimpers that escape him. *His pain is tearing me apart.* Hurrying up the steps, I open the clinic door and rush inside. When Ruth, the secretary sees me her eyes widen and she shouts, "Doctor Vale! We have an emergency out front!"

Doctor Sean Vale comes running and asks, "What have we got?"

"Rabbit shifter got caught in a bear trap. He's lost a lot of blood and his hind leg is fucked up." Thank the gods Sean has studied both human and animal medicine otherwise he wouldn't be able to help my mate unless he shifts. With the amount of pain he's in I don't see that happening unless he's forced to.

Sean waves me over and says, "Follow me to a room so I can assess the damage."

Nodding, I follow Sean down the hall to an empty exam room and place the rabbit on the bed. Sean asks a nurse to bring in some blood and pain medication. Once the nurse has the rabbit hooked up to an I.V and starts the blood transfusion, Sean administers the pain medication then gets to work examining the wound.

After he's finished, he says, "Nice job on the tourniquet Everett. You likely saved this shifter's life. He's going to need surgery to fix his leg. Not only is the bone shattered but the wounds from the teeth of the trap are deep and cut into the muscle." Then to the nurse he says, "Let's get him put under and into the operating room immediately."

Stroking the rabbit's fur, I ask Sean, "What's the outlook here?"

"It's hard to say until I get into the operating room. Worst case, he loses the leg. Best case, I get it fixed but he could end up walking with a limp for the rest of his life. I just can't be certain without getting a look at the internal damage."

Feeling tears prick my eyes again, I nod. "I understand. Take good care of him okay? He's my mate and I don't want to lose him after just having found him."

Sean squeezes my shoulder reassuringly and says, "He's in good hands. If you want to get back to work, I'll have the nurse keep you updated."

I shake my head. "I'll wait in the lobby. I'm not leaving the building while he's here."

Sean smiles faintly. "I figured you'd say that. You can wait in this room if you'd like. I'll be bringing him back in here when he's out of surgery."

Nodding, I give the rabbit's fur one last stroke, then press a kiss to the top of his head and say, "I'll be right here waiting for you beautiful. The doctor is going to fix you up," then I step back so Sean and the nurse can get him prepped for surgery. When they disappear down the hall with him, I collapse in the chair, bury my face in my hands and pray to the fates. *Please let my mate be okay.*

CHAPTER THREE

Beep...beep...beep...Jesus where is that infernal noise coming from? It's annoying as hell. Memories of getting caught in that bear trap surge to the forefront of my mind and suddenly, I'm wide-awake wondering where I am and how I got here. The room I'm in is dark and the light of the moon is streaming through the blinds on the window. Turning my head to the left where the beeping is coming from, I see the machine keeping track of my heartrate. Looking down at myself, I see the I.V in my arm. My left leg is wrapped in bandages and has a metal brace with rods around it. *Okay, obviously I'm in some kind of hospital, but how did I get here?*

Vaguely, I recall someone helping me but the specifics of how it happened are lost thanks to the haze of pain I was in. Turning to my right, I see a man in a green police uniform asleep in the recliner in the corner. For a moment, I panic thinking I was somehow identified and he's here to keep me from trying to escape. Then, I remember I was in my rabbit form before I ended up here so unless he somehow found my pack there's no way he knows who I am.

That knowledge helps me relax and I let my gaze roam over the sleeping man. The moon shining through the blinds lights up his face. *Holy batman, he's gorgeous.* His short dark hair is tousled like he's been running his fingers through it constantly. The green uniform shirt is unbuttoned revealing the white undershirt underneath that's more of a crop top than an actual shirt because it's been torn. There's also a stain on it that looks like blood. *He must've been the one to help me, I wonder why he stayed.* Rolling my eyes at the stupid thought, I tell myself the uniform says it all. He probably stayed so he could question me.

The man shifts and I see the patch on the sleeve of his uniform shirt says 'Game Warden Alaska' instead of police. *I hope I don't get slapped with a trespassing charge since I was technically on someone's land when I got caught in that trap.* That would not be good for me considering what I was already facing. Shaking my head, I tell myself not to worry about it right now. I've got other things to tackle at the moment. Like the fact my mouth is drier than the Sahara and I desperately need to pee. *How the hell am I supposed to get out of this bed by myself?*

Gripping the bed rails, I try to shift myself so I can swing my legs over the side of the bed and yelp as pain shoots up my leg at the movement. The footrest on the recliner slams shut and suddenly the game warden is at my side. There's a smile on his face and his eyes convey his relief. "I'm glad to see you awake. Don't try to get up. Doc said you shouldn't be moving around yet."

"I've got to pee and I'm thirsty."

The man blushes, clears his throat, and says, "You have a catheter so you can just pee. I'll go see a nurse about getting you something to drink."

He buttons his uniform shirt and walks out of the room and I take the opportunity to pee. Doing so with a stranger in the room would've been humiliating and embarrassing so I'm thankful he thought to give me some privacy. The bright light from the open door makes me wince because it shows me how bad my leg really looks. *I don't think I'll be going anywhere anytime soon.* The man returns a few minutes later with a cup and he sets it on a tray while he helps me sit up so I can drink it.

Once I'm upright, I take the cup from him and sip the water through the straw. It's so damn refreshing. The man pulls a chair over to the bed and sits on it. "The doctor will be in to see you in the morning. He's left for the night already."

"What happened? I don't remember much after getting caught in the trap."

"A couple of kids looking for easter eggs found you in the trap. They thought you were the Easter bunny and panicked. Their mother contacted me, and I freed you from the trap then brought you here. The doc had to perform surgery on your leg to fix all the damage. Thankfully, you shifted when they put you under otherwise you would've had to stay in your rabbit form until you recovered completely. Sean says you should be fully healed within a week but may have to do some physical therapy to work the damaged muscles and make sure you don't end up walking with a limp for the rest of your life."

A week...I can't be lying in bed for a week. I need to find the wolf shifter councilman. The man smiles at me and says, "I can tell by the look on your face the thought of being indisposed for a week is not something that pleases you."

I nod. "You'd be right. I'm sorry, I didn't even think to ask your name."

"I'm Everett Michaelis and you are?"

"Cotton Daniels." *Shit...I probably shouldn't have given him my real name.*

Everett chuckles, "Cotton huh? It suits you. Can I ask what you were doing that close to sleuth lands?"

Staring at him in confusion, I ask, "I'm sorry, sleuth lands? What do you mean?"

Everett tilts his head and says, "You're not from around here, are you?"

I shake my head.

"Killua Mountain is home to a sleuth of bear shifters. You were pretty close to the sleuth's cabins when you got caught in the trap."

Wide-eyed, I blurt, "Why would bear shifters have bear traps so close to their homes?"

"Poachers set them. I recently closed the case, but the poachers refused to give an exact number of traps they set out so there's no way to know how many they put out. The sleuth enforcers have been searching the forest but obviously, they haven't found them all yet."

"I'm glad you caught them."

Everett nods and leans forward to rest his elbows on his knees. "I am too. What were you doing out there if you're not from this area?"

Unsure if I can trust him, I give him a portion of the truth. "I was just letting my rabbit out for a bit."

Everett frowns. "If that were the case, there are other places closer to town perfect for such an occasion. You would've known that if you stopped in town and asked around. Coming as far as sleuth lands like you did wouldn't have been necessary. What are you hiding from me, mate?"

I swear my eyes must be bugging out of my head when I ask, "What did you just call me?"

Everett's frown deepens. "You mean you haven't realized it yet? We're mates. I knew it when I scented your blood in the woods."

I shake my head. "Rabbit shifters aren't the best when it comes to scenting things."

Everett holds his arm out in front of my face and orders, "Sniff."

Gripping his wrist, I pull it to my nose and sniff him. His scent of woods, raspberries, and mint makes me want to bottle it and wear it as cologne. *Holy shit he's right. We're mates.* While the news does change things, I'm not ready to divulge everything. Just because we're mates it doesn't mean I can trust him implicitly. I'll have to get to know him first before I tell him about what led me to being on the run. Instead, I say, "I can't believe it. Of all the ways I could've met my mate, being caught in a bear trap was not one I would've imagined."

Everett laughs and says, "It's not what I'd have imagined either, but fate does work in mysterious ways. Now, will you answer my question? Please?"

Knowing as an officer of the law he won't let this go until I answer him, I say, "I didn't come through town. I was hiking through the forest. I printed a trail map I found online before I started the hike. I'd been on my way to Killua and didn't have far to go according to the map. When I took a break for food and water at lunch, I decided to let my rabbit out for a bit before continuing on to town then I got caught in the trap and here we are."

Everett's eyes light up when I tell him I'd been hiking and he asks, "Where'd you start?" I can tell by the expression on his face that he loves the thought of his mate enjoying nature as much as he obviously does as evidenced by his profession. Biting my lip, I tell him, "Well, my car broke down and fixing it probably would've cost more than the car was worth, so I junked it but instead of buying a new one, I went ahead and started my hike in Washington from the Okanogan Wenatchee National Forest."

Everett gapes at me, speechless and I try not to laugh because the look on his face is comical. Finally, he shakes his head and says, "I'm impressed. That's a massive distance to travel. How long did it take you to get this far?"

"Almost a month."

Everett whistles. "That's a helluva journey. Why didn't you just get on a plane?"

Damn...just my luck he'd ask something like that. The man isn't an idiot and it's a logical question. No normal person decides to hike that far instead of just getting a car or hopping on a plane. If I were in his shoes, I'd ask questions too. *Now, I need to figure out how to answer him without outright lying.* Sighing internally, I realize there's no way I can get away with not telling him everything no matter how much I wish I could.

CHAPTER FOUR

While I wait for Cotton to answer my question, I take a minute to admire him. Cotton is adorable with his short tousled gray hair, baby faced features partially hidden by the gray beard he's sporting, and sapphire eyes. He's thin like a dancer but still has muscle definition. It's hard to judge how tall he is with him lying in bed like this, but I believe he's only a few inches shy of my own six-foot-five height. The white gown he's wearing makes the bright colorful tattoo sleeves on his arms stand out even more. The designs are video game themed.

On his right forearm is Sonic the hedgehog looking like he's about to jump into the air. Above Sonic's head in the blue sky are floating mushrooms, stars, and a golden eagle-like bird. Under Sonic at his wrist are three small triangles making up a bigger triangle. His left arm is a mirror of the right only with Shadow, red turtle shells, and a grey bird. The work is amazing. Whoever did it is seriously talented. I've always believed tattoos should mean something to the person getting them so I can't help but wonder if there's a reason my mate got this specific design.

Finishing my perusal, I return my gaze to his face and see a number of emotions flicker across it. His face is like a book. Easy to read. From the moment we started talking, I could tell he was hiding something. The fact that he seemed fearful for a split second when I asked why he didn't get on a plane only proves my theory. I know us being mates isn't incentive enough for him to trust me with his secrets, but I find myself hoping he will. I'll do whatever it takes to keep him safe from whatever it is he's afraid of.

After a few minutes of silence, Cotton sucks in a deep breath as if to steel himself for what he's about to say. "I couldn't get on a plane because I would've had to present my I.D for a ticket and that would've given away my location and where I was headed."

"So, you're on the run from something or someone."

Cotton nods. "My herd alpha is after me for what he was told was an unprovoked attack on his son. I'm sure he's labeled me as a rogue, so I decided if I want to avoid jail or death, I'd have to go to the council myself and plead my case. I came to Killua to see if I can get the wolf shifter council member to listen to my side of things since they can scent lies."

Crossing my arms, I lean back in my chair and say, "It's not foolproof though. If the person telling the lie believes it to be true, it'll scent as truth."

Cotton sighs and picks at non-existent lint on the blanket. "I know that, but I figure if I tell my story it'll be enough for my herd alpha's son to be brought in for questioning and then hopefully, they'll catch him lying."

"Will you tell me what happened?"

Cotton shrugs and says, "He tried to rape me, so in order to get away I clubbed him over the head with a rock and ran. By the time I got close to my house, he'd already called his father on the phone and spun his story. My best friend was waiting for me in the woods with a bag of food, money, and some of my own things. He told me he'd put the rest of my stuff in storage and that I needed to get away because the enforcers were out looking for me. So, I ran. To avoid being tracked down, I emptied my bank account, bought a cheap car under an assumed name and headed this way. I'd only been on the road twenty-four hours when that cheap car bit the dust. You know the rest."

Cotton's tone is nonchalant like it's not a big deal that the herd alpha's son tried to rape him, but it *is* a big deal. If I get my hands on the little prick, I'll ring his neck for what he tried to do to my mate. Scooting my chair closer to the bed, I take his hand in mine and squeeze it. "I swear to you, we'll get this straightened out. I'll take you to meet Mason Mayweather myself as soon as Sean discharges you. There's no way in hell I'll let you go to jail for something you did in self-defense."

Cotton whips around to look at me so fast, I fear he's given himself whiplash. His gorgeous sapphire eyes are wide and brimming with unshed tears. "You mean, you aren't going to turn me in?"

"Of course not. You don't deserve to go to jail. I bet if word got out about the alpha's son, more people would come forward to speak against him. I seriously doubt you were the first one he's ever attacked, and the others probably weren't lucky enough to escape like you were."

Cotton looks down and nods. "I had the same thought. It's why I didn't go to the rabbit shifter council member. I wanted to be sure the person I spoke to knew for a fact I was telling the truth."

Winking at him, I say with a smile, "It's a good thing your mate is a bear then. Our sense of smell is better than a wolf's. When it's time to go in front of the full shifter council, you'll have me and Mason at your back to attest to the fact you're telling the truth. We'll get the herd alpha's son brought to justice, even if I have to go over the shifter council's head by asking my sleuth's alpha to contact the paranormal council for a fixer."

Cotton's mouth drops open in shock. "You'd do that for me?"

I nod. "Of course, I would. We're mates and mates take care of each other. Though even if we weren't mates, I'd still do it because I pride myself on helping those in need if I can."

Cotton smiles and says, "You're a good man."

Blushing, I shrug. "I try."

Resting against the pillows behind him, Cotton says, "Now that you know what I'm running from, let's change the subject. I'm a captive audience since I can't get up, which presents the perfect opportunity for us to get to know each other." With a teasing glint in his eyes, he winks and adds, "I can't run away if you bore me to death."

Barking out a laugh, I tell him, "I'll try my best not to bore you. What would you like to know?"

"What made you want to become a game warden?"

"I originally wanted to be a forest ranger, but I came across some poachers while running in my animal form as a kid and reported them to the game warden at the time. When they were caught, I was proud of myself for having a hand in it and decided that was what I wanted to do for the rest of my life. What about you? What do you do?"

Cotton's expression turns sad when he says, "I was a video game programmer but after being MIA for a month I'm certain I've lost my job."

The tattoos he's got make sense now.

"I'm sure we can find out and possibly get your job back if you did in fact lose it. I can contact them and spin a tale about you being in an accident and just coming out of a coma. I'm sure Sean will back me up if they require some kind of evidence."

Cotton nods. "Sounds good but let's wait until after I've recovered. This brace is bound to get in the way of a laptop, and I doubt I can sit at a desk with it to work on a desktop computer."

I shake my head. "No, I don't suppose you could. Tell me, how were you able to travel two thousand miles in the woods on foot and survive without going into any towns for supplies?"

Cotton laughs and says, "My dad is ex-military. He taught us kids how to live off the land. We'd go on trips into the woods during every season and every type of weather and he'd leave us there for a week. I loved it and would go on trips myself for vacation whenever I could. All I had to do was buy everything I'd need before I started because I left home in a hurry and didn't have time to take any of my supplies with me. I packed everything into the large backpack I bought and hunted for my food."

Grinning, I feel pride at how capable he is. "That's amazing, I look forward to going camping with you sometime."

Cotton smiles at me and says, "I'd like that," then after changing his position so he's sitting up better, he tells me, "You know, I'm curious about something. Why don't I stink? It's been a week since I had a chance to really bathe. I know I was rank before I shifted."

Feeling a blush creep up my cheeks to the tips of my ears, I say, "I um, gave you a sponge bath after you came back from surgery. The nurse was going to do it, but my bear wasn't having it."

Cotton blushes. "I see. Thank you for that. I suppose you'll have to help me with that until I'm able to have a real shower."

"I swear, I'll do whatever I can to help you. I probably should've mentioned this earlier, but I was so excited about you waking up, I forgot."

Cotton's left eyebrow raises, and he says, "Tell me what?"

Pointing to the little remote with the green button on it laying on the bed beside him, I say, "You're on a pain pump. You can press that button every fifteen minutes."

Cotton snatches up the remote and presses the button. "Oh, thank the gods, I thought I'd have to call for the nurse to bring it in."

Guilt stabs me and I tell him, "I'm sorry I didn't mention it earlier."

Cotton shakes his head and smiles at me reassuringly. "It's okay. I wasn't feeling much pain until I moved to get more comfortable just now. It was a dull ache but when I moved it was like someone inserted a hot fire poker through the bottom of my foot and shoved it up the length of my leg until it came out of my ass cheek. My poor ass, I'd rub it if I could."

I shouldn't laugh because he's in pain and it's not right, but I can't help it. The poor ass comment has me in stitches. Cotton glares at me but there's no heat behind it. "Go ahead, laugh at my pain, asshole."

Wiping tears from my eyes, I say, "I'm sorry, beautiful but I can't help it. If you want me to, I can rub your ass for you."

Cotton barks out a laugh and says, "Thanks for the offer but I'm good."

Shrugging, I say, "Okay, let me know if you change your mind."

Cotton winks. "Oh, I will. You can bet on that."

We trade more 'get to know you' questions back and forth until Cotton's eyes start to droop. Leaning over, I kiss his forehead and say, "Get some rest, beautiful. I'll be here when you wake up.

CHAPTER FIVE

I've just finished the breakfast Everett brought me after I sent him home to shower and change when the doctor comes in. He's a tall rail thin man with hair so blonde it's almost white. *I bet he blinds people when the sun hits it just right.* The thought has me biting back a laugh. Sean smiles at me and says, "Good morning. I'm happy to see you're awake and you seem to be in good spirits."

Returning his smile, I nod. "I've got a lot to be happy about. I'm not in pain. I just ate a fantastic breakfast, and I met my mate."

Sean nods. "That is a lot to be happy about. Since you seem to be doing so well, and if your leg looks good, I'll discharge you today. We'll do another X-ray this morning to see how you've healed so far so I can judge how soon the brace can be removed."

"Sounds good doc. Let's get this done." The nurse came in earlier and removed the catheter, so I'm able to go to the bathroom on my own with the use of crutches.

Sean laughs. "I like your tenacity." He transfers me to a wheelchair, and I wave at Everett, calling out, "I'll be right back," as Sean takes me to have my leg x-rayed. It only takes a few minutes for him to get the pictures he needs and soon I'm back in my room where Everett is still seated in the chair by the bed, looking delectable in a black t-shirt and jeans. *I hope this leg heals quickly so we can claim each other.* After getting to know him last night, I'm certain fate made the right choice in pairing us. I'm looking forward to spending the rest of my life with him. But first, I need to settle my past. The last thing I want is to get thrown in jail or worse and have the both of us lose our lives in the end.

Sean tells me, "I'll return after I've looked over the X-rays," and leaves the room.

Turning to Everett, I ask, "Did you speak with Mason?"

He nods. "I did. If Sean discharges you today, I'll take you to Mason's and he can hear your story from you before we go home."

Raising an eyebrow at him, I question, "Home?"

Everett blushes and rubs the back of his neck. "Forgive me, I shouldn't have assumed. If you don't want to come home to my cabin, I can check you into a hotel under an assumed name."

Reaching over, I grab his free hand and squeeze it. "Hush. Of course, I'll be going home with you. My attempt at teasing you fell a little flat that time."

Everett grins and it lights up his whole face. "I'm glad you'll be coming with me. You won't regret it, I promise."

"Babe, we're mates. I could never regret anything that involves you."

Everett brings our hands up and kisses the back of mine. "That's nice to hear. I swear, I'll do all I can to make you happy."

Winking at him, I say, "Of that, I have no doubt."

Sean returns and the grin on his face has my shoulders sagging in relief. I didn't realize how tense I was until now. Sean states, "Good news. You can go home today. Your leg is healing nicely. You'll only have to keep the brace and use crutches for two more days. After that, we'll take the brace off and you can use a cane until the leg is completely healed. I was able to stitch the muscles back together for them to heal so I'm confident you won't have a permanent limp when you walk. I expect you'll be back to normal by the end of the week."

Grinning, I hold out my hand for him to shake and say, "Thank you doc. That's fantastic news."

Sean shakes my hand and says, "I'll get your discharge papers ready and get you some oral painkillers to take with you if you end up needing them."

I thank him again and he leaves. Once he's gone, Everett holds up a bag and says, "I brought some clothes for you. It's just one of my t-shirts and a pair of athletic shorts. I figured you wouldn't want to leave the hospital in that gown."

"You'd be right. Hand me the shorts and I'll put those on now."

Everett hands me the bag and I pull the shorts out then carefully turn so I'm sitting on the edge of the bed. I'm trying to figure out how I'll get them over my injured leg since I can't bend it when Everett comes around to where I am and says, "I can help you with that."

I let him take the shorts and he carefully puts them on me. When he's got them up as far as they'll go, I hop off the bed, taking care not to let my braced leg touch the floor and Everett pulls the shorts up the rest of the way, tying the strings tight so they won't slip off my hips. With the shorts on, I sit back down on the bed to wait for the nurse to come in and remove the I.V. and other wires I'm hooked to so I can put the shirt on and get out of this gown. The material is scratchy, and I'm ready to get it off.

Feeling impatient, I press the call button and ask the nurse to come take out my I.V. Now that I'm allowed to go, I'm anxious to get out of here. Being confined to this room and this bed isn't my idea of a good time and I'd rather not spend any more time here than is absolutely necessary. Finally, the nurse comes in and removes the I.V. needle. When I'm free of all the wires, I whip the gown off and pull on the t-shirt. There was a lone flip flop in the bag as well and I'm thankful Everett thought to put it in there since I'll need something to wear on my right foot on the way out of here.

I put the sandal on my foot and hop off the bed again, tucking my crutches under my arms. Sean comes in with my discharge papers and a pill bottle with my name on it. After signing the papers, I hand them, and the pill bottle off to Everett since I can't carry them. "Thank you for taking care of me."

Sean says, "Just doing my job."

"Still, thank you."

"You're welcome," then with a wink he adds, "I won't make you ride out of here in a wheelchair."

Laughing, I thank him again and turn to Everett and whisper conspiratorially, "Let's get out of here before he changes his mind."

Everett chuckles and I follow him out of the room. We say our goodbyes to the staff we pass until we get outside. Taking in a deep breath, I enjoy the fresh air and say, "Hello freedom," making Everett laugh. He kisses my cheek and says, "Wait here, I'll go get my truck and bring it around. I think it'll be easier and more comfortable for you to ride in the backseat since it's a bench seat and you can stretch your leg across it."

I watch him dart across the street to a parking lot where he gets into a black truck that has a police light bar on top and stickers marking it as a game warden's vehicle. Soon, Everett parks the truck in front of the clinic and hops out. He opens the back door for me and says, "Let me help you in."

I hobble over and turn my back to the seat. Everett puts his hands on my hips and lifts me onto the seat. I scoot across the seat until my back is against the other door. Reaching behind me, I grab the seatbelt and put it on even though the way it comes across me is awkward with the position I'm sitting in. Everett asks, "You good?" At my nod, he closes the door and gets in the truck.

As he pulls out into traffic, I ask, "So, where to now?"

Everett looks at me in the rearview mirror and says, "Now, we go see Mason."

CHAPTER SIX

Mason lives in a cabin on a hill just outside of town. It's a ten-minute drive from the clinic. Since Mason is expecting us, I don't get stopped by the guard stationed at the entrance of his driveway. I park my truck in front of the porch. A feat that wouldn't be possible if Mason didn't have a circular driveway. Cutting the engine, I pocket the keys and hop out, circling around the truck to the passenger side. Opening the door, I wait for Cotton to scoot across the seat then help him down. Handing him his crutches, I let him go up the porch stairs first so I'm there to catch him if he falls.

Mason's cabin is more like a log mansion. It's two stories with a covered wrap around porch on both levels and is entirely self-sustaining. Mason doesn't like to come into town much. Usually, it's only to get the supplies he needs that he doesn't grow or make himself. He's the quintessential mountain man and I've always wondered if his position as a councilman is the reason he isolates himself so much or if something in his past is the cause. I might consider him a friend, but I don't know him well enough to pry into his life. I figure if he wants me to know, he'll tell me himself.

Cotton rings Mason's doorbell and the housekeeper answers the door. Smiling, I say, "Hello Bridget, we're here to see Mason."

Bridget is a brown-haired sprite of a woman and is the sole proprietor of the town's cleaning service. With a smile, she waves us in and says, "Come in, he's in his office."

We follow her through the cabin to Mason's office. Mason is leaned back in his leather chair and has his feet propped up on the desk. He's talking to someone on the phone and throwing a tennis ball at the wall that bounces back into his hands each time. Two other men are in the room with him. There's one on the left in the corner behind his chair and one on the right. We sit in the chairs across from his desk and wait for him to finish his call.

Five minutes later, Mason hangs up the phone, drops his feet from his desk and spins the chair so he's facing us. Mason looks like an Irish lumberjack with his bushy red beard, untamed curly red hair, and flannel shirt. Mason says, "It's good to see you again Everett. I take it this little cutie is the mate you were telling me about?" Mason's eyes twinkle with amusement at Cotton's blush.

Chuckling, I tell him, "Yes, this is Cotton."

Mason stands and reaches across the desk to hold out his hand for a shake, so Cotton doesn't have to stand again. Cotton shakes his hand and Mason says, "It's a pleasure to meet you, Cotton."

"Likewise."

Mason returns to his seat and says, "I made some inquiries after we spoke yesterday Everett. Your mate has indeed been labelled a rogue and charged with an unprovoked attack. There's currently a warrant out for his arrest with the council. Since he's here I'm technically supposed to report him but I'm not going to. Instead, I'm going to video Cotton relaying his side of things and will send it with the statement that Cotton is filing his own charges against his former herd alpha's son."

Cotton asks, "Is that a good idea? Won't it reveal to them where I am?"

Mason nods. "It will, but I'll make it clear you're under my protection and will not be arrested without an investigation into what really happened."

Cotton's shoulders sag. "I'm not sure I'm comfortable with this. If the alpha gets wind of my location, he'll send his enforcers after me to have me brought back so he can dispense justice without the council's input."

Mason nods in understanding. "I get it why you're worried. It's my hope that it won't come to that but if it does, you've got Everett to protect you. I'll even send a couple of my guards to sleuth lands to guard you as well if it'll make you feel better."

Cotton turns to me and asks, "What do you think? Do we need the extra guards?"

Thinking on it a moment, I nod my head. "It would be an extra line of defense. I'm confident I can protect you myself but with others keeping an eye out we could catch them before they have a chance to get to us."

Mason tells him, "It's my hope that your statement along with the charges we're filing will be enough to have the herd alpha's son brought in for questioning. I've sent an investigator to the herd territory to make subtle inquiries among the herd's members to see if we can find others willing to come forward. If I have statements from others to go with yours it'll show a pattern and will make the case against Peter ironclad. I hope to hear from him by tomorrow. I have zero tolerance for assholes and will do all I can to see that you get justice. Now, let's get started, shall we?"

Cotton's eyes widen and he nods. One of the other men in the room sets up a camera and starts filming as Mason asks Cotton to tell us what happened. Cotton retells his story and answers Mason's questions. The whole thing only takes about ten minutes and when finished, Mason says, "I'll send this in as soon as I hear back from my investigator. I swear we'll get justice for you Cotton. No one should have to go through what you did."

I hope Peter gets exactly what he deserves. Bastard.

Cotton bites his lip, tears pricking his eyelids as he nods. "Thank you."

Mason smiles at him and says, "You're welcome. Did you guys want to stick around for a bit? My chef will be preparing lunch and it's usually something delicious if you'd like to join me for a bite."

Looking at Cotton, I raise an eyebrow and ask, "What do you think?"

Cotton shakes his head and says to Mason. "Maybe another time. I'd like to go home and put my leg up. Thank you for the offer."

Mason smiles and says, "Of course. My door is always open so stop by anytime. I always welcome the company of friends." The 'it's other people I don't like dealing with' goes unsaid.

Standing, I shake Mason's hand and tell him, "We'll take you up on that sometime soon."

"I'll keep you updated on the investigation."

"We'd appreciate that."

Mason says, "Let me walk you out," and comes around his desk. Cotton and I follow him out. When we get to the door, we shake hands with him again and thank him for his help before walking out. I descend the stairs first so I can catch Cotton if he falls forward. He's become an expert at the crutches already, so he easily navigates the steps without issue.

After helping him into the truck, I take us home. When he's feeling better, I'll take him back into town and show him around. My cabin is a modest three-bedroom, two-bathroom, single story affair with a covered porch on the front and back. The porch doesn't have steps, but it does have a swing I love to sit on in the evenings when the weather is warm. My mother planted flowers in the window boxes for me because she felt my cabin needed something pretty and I'm not the best at gardening.

I've got a root cellar under the house where my generator is stored. I've got non-perishable food and other supplies like wood, water, candles, fuel, and batteries. With winters in Alaska being harsh as hell, it's best to be prepared. If snow drifts get too high it would be impossible for me to go out to my woodshed to restock the stack on the back porch if I happened to run out, so I keep an emergency stash in the root cellar.

I back my truck into my little driveway at the side of the cabin so the door Cotton will be getting out of is closest to the porch. After helping Cotton from the vehicle, I lead him into the cabin. All my furniture is rustic looking because it's handmade from reclaimed wood. One of the sleuth members has a furniture making business and outfits everyone's houses to their liking. All of my furniture has bears, forests, and other woodland creatures carved into it with a layer of resin over each design, so nothing ruins the carvings. The couch has to be one of my most favorite pieces because despite it being made from wood and designed like a bench, the cushions on it are so comfortable it feels like you're sitting on a cloud. I ended up buying the chairs to match.

Cotton spots his bag in one of the chairs and looks at me over his shoulder. "You found my pack?"

I shake my head. "I didn't. While you were sleeping last night, I sent a text message and asked my friend who's the sleuth's tracker to follow your scent from the trap and find your things. It didn't take him long to find it and he dropped it off when I came back to shower and change clothes this morning. I didn't want to go through your things without your permission so instead of grabbing your own clothes I gave you some of mine."

Cotton smiles and says, "My clothes were dirty anyways so it wouldn't have mattered if you did go through my stuff."

"If you want, I can throw your things in my washing machine."

Cotton nods. "I'd like that. I won't be able to wear the pants for a while, but it'll be nice to have my own t-shirts." *Damn...I liked the sight of him in my clothes.*

Seeing my expression, Cotton laughs and says, "I know you like me wearing your things, that much is obvious, but if you haven't noticed you're a bit wider than I am. I feel like a child playing dress-up with the way this shirt keeps sliding down and revealing my shoulders. I wouldn't mind sleeping in your shirt when it smells like you if I'm home alone but any other time, I'd prefer my own clothes."

Smiling at him, I kiss his forehead and say, "I understand. I'll take care of the laundry while you put your leg up."

"Thank you."

"No problem."

Cotton makes his way over to the couch and sits down. Grabbing one of the throw pillows, I put it on the coffee table and bring it closer to the couch so he can put his leg on it. Cotton looks around and says, "You have a nice place."

"Thank you. I'm glad you like it since it'll be your place too once we claim each other."

When his gaze lands on the wicker basket next to one of the chairs, he turns to me with a raised eyebrow and asks, "Do you knit?"

Blushing, I tell him, "Actually, I crochet. For me it's easier than knitting. I know it's the kind of thing grandmas do, but I find it relaxing. Right now, I'm working on a couple baby blankets. I'm going to give them to the sleuth members that are expecting babies this year."

Cotton grins. "Aw that's sweet of you. I think it's nice that you have a hobby that relaxes you even if it's something grandmas usually do. I don't have any hobbies like that. Maybe now that I'm not working, I can find something I like to do."

"I'll help you in any way I can. If you want someone to try new things with, I'm your man."

With a wink, he says, "You sure are," making me laugh at the not-so-subtle innuendo. Shaking my head, I hand him the television remote, kiss the top of his head, and grab his pack from the chair to take into the laundry room with me. I unpack everything on the laundry table where I normally fold my clothes. I chuck his clothes and bed linens into the washing machine and start it then I finish unpacking everything else. When I get to the bottom of the bag and find multiple stacks of cash, I call out, "Cotton, what should I do with the money in your bag?"

Cotton calls back, "Just hide it somewhere no one is going to find it. I trust you."

Gathering the cash, I take it into the bedroom and crawl under the bed with it. Lifting the floorboards hiding my safe, I input the combination and put his money inside it. Returning everything to its place, I slide out from under the bed bringing dust bunnies with me and return to the laundry room where I gather his camping supplies and take them to the shed out back. *I look forward to the day when he can retrieve all of his things and mix them in with mine. This will really be his home then.*

CHAPTER SEVEN

Five Days Later...

Walking out of the clinic, I shout, "I'm freeee, free from the cane," to the tune of *Free Fallin' by Tom Petty* making Everett double over laughing. Today was my final check up with Sean. I'm fully healed and no longer have to use a cane. Best of all, Sean was right about me not having permanent damage to my muscles, so I don't walk with a limp. Over the past few days, I've enjoyed making Everett laugh. Aside from my friend Keenan, he's the only one who gets my jokes and doesn't criticize me when I do things like what I just did. People back home would've asked me when I'm going to grow up and stop acting like a fool instead of laughing like Everett.

Everett took two weeks off from his job so he could take care of me. We've got one more week together before he has to go back, and I plan to make the most of it. Looking over my shoulder at Everett, I say, "Let's grab lunch. I'm starving."

Everett chuckles. "You're always hungry."

Shrugging, I tease, "I'm a growing boy."

Everett rolls his eyes and shakes his head. "You're something alright."

Laughing, I take his hand and practically drag him down the street to the local diner. Pushing open the door to the diner, I drag him over to the counter so we can place a to-go order. As much as I'd love to sit at a table and eat with him, I've got other plans in mind for today. Namely, us taking this food home and likely having to reheat it because I'm ready for us to claim each other. Hell, if I'm being truthful, I was ready for this days ago, but Everett refused to possibly hinder my recovery, so I've had to wait until I got the all-clear from Sean. Once I get Everett home, I'm going to drag him into the bedroom and not let him out until I've succeeded in us completing our bond.

In the back of my mind, I do worry about what's going to happen with the Peter situation, but I've been assured by Mason he'll push to have me put on house arrest if I am found guilty of an unprovoked attack at the hearing next week. Though he doesn't think it'll happen since the evidence his investigator has gathered against Peter is astronomically overwhelming. Over twenty herd members came forward and made statements. The number honestly shocked me, and I can't help but wonder how many of those people went to the alpha only for him to shove the truth under the rug. *I hope the herd alpha gets thrown in jail too. There's no way he isn't aware of the kind of person his son is.*

Everett's voice asking, "Are you alright," brings me out of my musings. Smiling at him I nod, "I'm fine."

We both order a burger and fries. He gets a soda with his and I get a vanilla milkshake. Once our food is ready, we leave the diner and make the trek back to his truck. As Everett drives us home, I watch the scenery pass by out the window. The smell of the food has my stomach growling loudly and I feel myself blush. It sounds like an angry bear. *Damn...I didn't think I was that hungry.* Pulling my fries from the bag, I stuff a couple into my mouth unconcerned by the fact that they're hot until they hit my tongue. Breathing through my mouth while fanning my face with my hand, I try to cool the fries currently burning my tastebuds off.

Everett laughs and teases, "Hey, beautiful, those fries are hot."

Finally swallowing them, I turn to look at him with wide-eyes. Feigning shock, I say sarcastically,

"They are? I hadn't noticed," making him laugh harder. Shaking my head, I finish off my fries. I'm about to devour the burger too when he parks the truck by our house. Grabbing the bag, I hop out and follow Everett inside. Sitting at the table, I remove the rest of the food from the bag and pass Everett. His stomach is now growling as loud as mine was making it obvious we should finish lunch first before any claiming can happen. Hunger isn't sexy and we'd get nowhere with our stomachs growling like they are.

We eat in silence and when we've finished, Everett asks, "So, now that you're fully healed want to go for a hike with me? We can let our animal forms out to play."

Grinning, I tell him, "I'd love to. Another day. Right now, I've got other plans."

He raises an eyebrow and questions, "Oh? And what would they be?"

Standing, I circle the table and pull him from his chair. Dragging him down the hall to our bedroom, I shove him back onto the bed and say, "We're not leaving this room until both of us are claimed."

Everett grins. "I can get behind that."

Chuckling, I lean down and kiss his lips, "I'm glad you're agreeable to my plan."

"What would you have done if I wasn't agreeable?"

Lifting his shirt over his head, I shrug and say, "Bribed you, probably. Or begged, depending on my mood. Now, if I was feeling kinky, I'd tie you up and torture you sexually until you gave in."

Whipping off my own shirt, I move off Everett so I can get my pants off. Everett kicks off his jeans and slides up the bed until his head is resting on the pillows. He grabs the lube from the nightstand and tosses it to me, then stuffs a pillow under his hips. Raising an eyebrow at him, I question, "What, no foreplay?"

"Consider the past five days of teasing touches and make out sessions foreplay. I've never been so on edge. We can do the slow body exploration later, right now I just want you to claim me so I can do the same to you."

Winking at him, I say, "Your wish is my command," and crawl onto the bed until I'm on my knees between his legs. I know he wants me to just get right to prepping him, but I can't resist exploring the tantalizing skin in front of me a little. Leaning over him, I start with his lips and kiss my way down his neck to his chest where I nip and suck each nipple before continuing my descent. His little growls of frustration are the cutest fucking thing I've ever heard. *I'll have to disobey his orders to skip foreplay more often if this is the response I get.* When I reach his hard cock, I kiss the tip before I take it into my mouth. While I'm sucking him slowly like I'm taking a leisure stroll through a park I open the lube and pour some onto my fingers.

Circling his hole, I push one finger inside and spread the lube around until he's able to take a second and then a third. Certain he's ready for me, I let his cock fall from my lips and move into position.

With the tip of my cock notched at his entrance, I ask, "Ready to be mine?"

Everett nods. "Been ready since the moment we met, beautiful. Make me yours."

Grinning down at him, I press my lips to his and say, "With pleasure," as I slowly push inside him. Everett's mouth forms an adorable little 'o' when he moans. When he's taken all of me, I give him some time to adjust before slowly retreating. Pushing forward again, I set a steady rhythm, taking it slow for a bit before I increase the pace. Everett's blunt nails dig into my back making a shiver of pleasure run through me.

As I begin to peg his prostate on each thrust, Everett gets more vocal, moaning and muttering nonsense like he's speaking in tongues. I'd laugh if I wasn't so lost in the bliss of us finally coming together like this. Feeling my orgasm getting closer, I reach between us and grip Everett's cock, stroking it in time with my thrusts to get Everett over the edge first. When it hits, Everett shouts, "Cotton," as he paints our chests with come. The tightening of his chute muscles around my cock rips my orgasm from me so forcefully my eyes nearly roll back into my head. Feeling my rabbit half surge forward, I give in to instinct and sink my teeth into Everett's neck, marking him as mine.

I grin around the wound when more come fills the space between us. Taking a couple sips of his blood, I pull away and seal the wound. Looking down into his blissed-out emerald eyes, I whisper fondly, "There's no getting rid of me now, babe. You're stuck with me."

Everett chuckles and presses his lips to mine. "I wouldn't have it any other way," then he rolls us so I'm the one under him and says, "Now, I get to return the favor."

Holding my arms out I say dramatically, "Take me, I'm yours."

"Oh, I intend to."

CHAPTER EIGHT

I'm woken by the sound of glass breaking and what sounds like a hushed argument between two people. Looking at the alarm clock on my nightstand, I see it's three in the morning. Cotton is tucked against my side and none of the sleuth members would just enter my house without knocking. Which means, whoever is inside isn't here for a friendly visit. Slipping from bed, I pull on my jeans from yesterday and grab my sidearm from the holster on the nightstand. Flicking the safety off, I make sure there's a bullet in the chamber. Hearing a startled squeak, I turn my head and see Cotton looking at me with eyes that are wide and full of fear. Putting a finger to my lips in the universal 'be quiet' gesture, I whisper, "Someone's in the house. Stay here while I go check it out."

Cotton leaps from bed and shakes his head. "No way. I'm not letting you go out there alone." He quickly pulls on his own jeans and grabs the bow and arrows he stashed in the corner of the bedroom. Instead of letting me put them in the root cellar with his other camping supplies, he decided they should be within reach in case his ex-alpha and the man's son got wind of where he's at. *Seems he was right to be paranoid about it.*

The doorknob to our bedroom door begins to turn and I raise my gun while Cotton notches back an arrow. Together, we aim our weapons at the door. When it flies open, revealing two men dressed head to toe in black, armed with guns and wearing ski-masks over their faces. Before they can get a shot off, I fire, hitting one in the hand so he can't hold the gun anymore, before I fire a second one to his kneecap so he's incapacitated and can't attack us with his bare hands. Cotton lets his arrow loose, nailing the other one in the shoulder so he drops his gun. Cotton then notches another arrow and aims for the leg like I did, dropping the second would-be assailant to the ground. Leaving the intruders to writhe on the floor in pain, I go into my closet and grab the blue ropes I have hanging in the back.

Exiting the closet, I toss one strand to Cotton and say, "Let's tie them up. The shots will have drawn attention and we don't want them to try and escape before the enforcers show up. Not that I believe they'll be going anywhere, but it's best to be on the safe side."

Cotton eyes the rope I tossed him and says teasingly, "You'll have to explain why you have these in your closet later."

Blushing, I flip him a middle finger and get to work tying up the intruder I shot. Once they're tied up, we drag them down the hall into the living room, where we flip on the lights right as the enforcers burst in from the front and back doors. The sleuth's alpha is hot on their heels dressed in a pair of rainbow unicorn baker pajama pants that say, 'I made you a batch of shut the fucupcakes,' and looking like he just rolled out of bed. Considering the late hour, I know that's exactly what he did. The big man wearing those pants would be hilarious in any other situation but not tonight.

Alpha Carson crosses his arms and asks with a booming voice, "What the hell is going on here?"

I point at the two men on the floor and say, "These two broke in with guns. I suspect they were here to kill my mate but one of them knocked that lamp off the end table and the sound of it breaking woke us. Which is how we were able to get the drop on them."

Alpha Carson says, "Well, let's see who was stupid enough to come after members of my sleuth," and rips the ski-masks from the men's heads. From their yowls, I suspect he took some hairs with the fabric. At Cotton's sudden inhalation, I realize these men must be from his herd. Alpha Carson, having heard, asks Cotton, "Do you know these two?"

Cotton nods. "That's my ex-alpha and his son. There's a council hearing next week to address the charges we've brought against each other. I guess they thought if they killed me, the charges and accompanying evidence against Peter would disappear."

The guilty looks on their faces tell us that's exactly what they were hoping for. Cotton's ex-alpha snarls, "It would've worked too. With you gone and a little money placed in the right hands, Peter would've been acquitted of the charges and be free to take over the herd like he's supposed to."

Cotton scoffs and rolls his eyes. "Free to hurt more people you mean. Even if you killed me and greased some palms, Peter wouldn't have gotten free of the charges. Not for long. You can't bury the statements of twenty plus victims without someone getting suspicious. I can guarantee that if you tried, the paranormal council would be knocking at your door eventually and those twenty-plus victims would be all too happy to come forward once again. Face it, your son is going down like he deserves and now, you're going to join him."

Turning to Alpha Carson, Cotton asks, "Will you call Councilman Mason and have him send some guards to retrieve these two? I'm done dealing with them and want them out of the house so Everett and I can clean up. I'd say the clean-up can wait until daylight, but the bloodstain is going to be a pain in the ass to get out of the wood floors if allowed to sit too long."

At Cotton's mention of guards, I'm reminded of the ones Mason had stationed around the house to protect us. Before Alpha Carson can respond to Cotton's question I add, "And have a couple of the enforcers search the area around the house for the guards Mason had on us. I figure these two did something to them in order to get access to the house."

Alpha Carson nods and signals a couple enforcers who leave the house to search then says, "We'll transfer these two to the cells in the basement of the main house to await the council guards." Another set of enforcers step forward and jerk the two men off the floor, hustling them out of the house amidst yowls of pain and protest. When they're gone, Alpha Carson says, "I'm glad the two of you weren't hurt. I'll let you know what I find out about the missing council guards."

Nodding, I say, "Thank you, alpha."

He crosses his arms and raises an eyebrow. "How many times have I told you to call me Carson? You know I don't stand on formality."

Laughing, I punch his shoulder like friends do, and say, "Truthfully, I lost count but as one of your best friends it's my job to irritate you a little."

"I thought that was the job of little brothers."

Cotton laughs and says, "He's got a point there, babe."

Shrugging, I say, "Maybe so, but considering we're as close as brothers, it's a moot point."

Carson barks out a laugh and slaps my arm. "You're right. Well, I'll be getting out of your hair now. You two get some rest. You've had quite the ordeal tonight. Don't worry about cleaning up, I'll have someone come over during the day to take care of it for you."

I shake my head. "Thanks for the offer, but we can manage the cleanup. Besides, I don't think I could sleep with the smell of blood permeating our bedroom."

"I understand. If you can't get all of it out of your hardwood floors, let me know and I'll have the sleuth's contractor come in and refinish the floors for you, free of charge."

Cotton says, "We'd appreciate that, thank you."

With a nod and a "No problem," from Carson, he and the rest of the enforcers leave. When the door closes behind them, I look at the blood streaked across the floor, and sigh, "I'll get the mop bucket and fill it with water."

"And I'll get the cleaning supplies."

It's going to be a long night.

CHAPTER NINE

Once we finished cleaning the blood from the floors, which took almost two hours because some of it had started to dry, Everett and I went back to bed only for sleep to elude us both. By the time eight o'clock rolls around, we've long since given up on sleep and choose to finally start the day instead of continuing to lay in bed awake. We probably could've passed the time with some pleasurable fun but neither of us was in the mood for it, so we cuddled and talked to each other about random things and childhood stories. I couldn't help but laugh when Everett told me about the time he ran in the woods as a bear for the first time and ended up on the wrong end of a family of skunks. It took five baths before his mother got the smell out of his fur.

After showering together, Everett and I dress then head into the kitchen. While I'm fixing us a quick but filling breakfast of overstuffed omelets, Everett calls the alpha to get an update on things. Everett puts the call on speaker so I can be a part of the conversation if I need to.

"Good morning, Everett."

"Morning, Carson. I'm calling to get an update."

Carson chuckles, "I figured that's what you were calling for. The enforcers found the missing guards. They'd been hit over the head and stashed in the woods behind your house. Aside from a headache, they'll be fine. As for the prisoners, the council guards just left with them. They'll be taken straight to the council jail to await trial."

I feel a weight lift off my shoulders at his words. *It's really over.* Now, I need to get through the hearing next week without landing in jail and everything will be right as rain.

Everett says, "I'm glad to hear that. So, what happens now?"

"Now, all that's left is for Cotton to go to his hearing next week. Mason will be collecting statements from myself and the enforcers in the room last night to add to the evidence he already has. Cotton's hearing is just a formality at this point. I highly doubt he'll be sentenced." *One can only hope.*

"I hope you're right Carson. Thanks for the update."

"No problem."

Everett ends the call as I plate up the food. Setting one in front of Everett, I take mine and sit in the seat across from him. After a few bites, I ask, "So, what are our plans for today?"

Everett swallows his bite of omelet and says, "I was thinking we could go for a run in the woods. Let our animal halves out to play for a bit. Just do something fun to take our minds off everything that's happened since last night."

Smiling at him, I say, "I'd like that. I think a stress-free day is exactly what we need."

"Then we'll head out after we finish eating."

"Sounds good."

The excitement of running in the woods with Everett has me devouring my omelet in record time. Everett seems to be just as excited as I am because he does the same. We leave the plates on the table to wash later and race to the back door, stripping as we go. Once we hit the back porch, I let Everett shift first. Soon, a large black bear is standing in his place and I can't resist the opportunity to run my fingers through his wiry fur. Everett makes a chuffing noise and bumps his head against my belly making me laugh. "Alright, alright, I get it." With one last scratch to his ears, I step back and initiate my shift.

Leaping off the porch I dart into the woods with Everett right behind me. As a shifter sized Flemish giant rabbit shifter, I'm pretty fast in animal form which will make for a fun game of chase. I can feel Everett's happiness through our bond and I'm sure he can feel mine.

This is exactly what we needed.

Most definitely.

Hearing his voice in my head for the first time shocks me into stopping and I tumble ass over teakettle through the brush and down a small hill where I roll through a raspberry bush before coming to a stop flat on my back looking at the sky. Seconds later, the view is blocked out by Everett's furry face. *Are you okay?*

I'm peachy.

Are you sure? I can see the amusement in his eyes when his next thought comes through. *You look like you got into a fight with a raspberry and the raspberry won.*

I'll have you know it was a bush and it did not win, thank you very much.

It kind of looks like it did, beautiful. Your fur is stained red. I'd think it was blood if I couldn't smell the raspberries on you.

Narrowing my eyes at him in my best glare impression, I stand on my back legs, bop him on the nose with the front one and take off running.

Tag, you're it!

I hear Everett laughing through our mind link as he chases me down. Leaping over logs and diving under bushes, I do my best to evade him. If rabbits could grin, I'd have a big one on my face right now. I've never been this happy and I look forward to more days like this one. I know there are things I still need to figure out, like if I want to try getting my job back at the gaming company and if I don't, what I'll do instead. Then there's the task of getting Keenan to send my stuff here from Nebraska. But those are things I'll worry about addressing on a different day.

Feeling a tap on my behind, I curse myself for getting distracted and letting Everett catch up.

Tag, you're it!

Everett rushes past me deeper into the forest and I think to myself *Oh, it's on* as I take off after him. Over an hour later, we stop at a stream to drink some water and rest before we start another game of chase. When lunch time rolls around, we decide to forage for things to eat since we're not ready to go home and end our day of fun just yet. I return to the raspberry bush I rolled through and eat the berries off it while Everett eats the fish he catches in the stream. We spend the rest of the day playing tag and exploring the woods. The sun is setting when we finally make our way home.

I had the best day babe. Thank you for suggesting it.

It was fun and one of the best days I've had in a while. We'll have to do it again soon.

I look forward to it.

As do I.

Race you home? Last one to the porch has to cook dinner.

You're on.

EPILOGUE

One week later...

I walk into the room where the hearing is being held with Cotton at my side. He's squeezing my hand so tightly I know he's nervous. Leaning over I whisper in his ear, "Everything is going to be alright."

"I hope so."

We sit at the unoccupied table on the left of the council chamber. On the right, dressed in orange jumpsuits and cuffed to the table and their seats are Cotton's ex-alpha and his son. There's an armed guard standing nearby in case they somehow manage to get free of their bonds. In front of us is a five-foot-tall raised semi-circle desk that each councilmember is seated behind. Since Cotton, his ex-alpha, and the alpha's son are all rabbits, the rabbit representative will speak for the council as a whole when relaying their decision. Because this isn't an actual trial but a preliminary hearing to decide if the council will proceed with the charges against Cotton, we don't have to plead our case through a lawyer as the evidence has already been presented for the council to review.

The rabbit representative clears her throat and says, "I won't keep you waiting. After reviewing the evidence presented by both parties, the council has decided to drop all charges against one Cotton Daniels on the grounds that he acted in self-defense and declare that he is not a rogue shifter." Cotton lets out a relieved breath and smiles.

The rabbit representative smiles at Cotton briefly before her expression turns serious again. "As for the charges Councilman Mason has filed on behalf of Cotton Daniels and twenty-two others against Peter and Jasper Smith, we'll be moving forward with those. Peter will be charged with multiple counts of rape and assault, one count of attempted rape, two counts of attempted murder, two counts of assault with a deadly weapon, and one count of breaking and entering. Jasper will be charged with obstruction of justice, multiple counts of accessory to rape, two counts of attempted murder, two counts of assault with a deadly weapon, and one count of breaking and entering. Both of you will remain in the council jail until a trial date is determined."

She slams the gavel down until the Smiths' protests quiet. Then, she clasps her hands and glares at the Smith men. "I have never been more disgusted by someone of my own species as I am by the two of you. I'd have you both killed where you sit for the pain you've caused so many if I could, but protocol demands you get a fair trial. Guards, escort them back to their cells."

Once they're taken from the room, the rabbit representative turns to Cotton and says, "Mr. Daniels, while I wish you'd have come to me with this, I understand why you went to Mason. A new alpha will be appointed to your former herd and he will be paying you and the other victims restitution from the Smiths' accounts. You'll be receiving a check in the mail sometime over the next few weeks."

Cotton shakes his head and says, "I don't want any money. You can give my portion to the other victims. The fact that neither of the Smith men can hurt anyone else because they're behind bars is enough for me in restitution."

"Duly noted. Well, that concludes this hearing. Mr. Daniels, you're free to go."

Cotton's smile is beaming when he says, "Thank you." With a wave to the council members, we stand and walk out of the council chambers so the next hearing can start. When the doors close behind us, I turn to Cotton to ask him if he wants to go get lunch, only I don't get the chance because he shouts, "Kee! What are you doing here?"

Following his line of sight, I see a tall rail-thin man with sandy blond hair and glasses walking towards us, a big smile on his face. "When I got your email about this hearing, I hopped on the first flight I could get. I'd have been here sooner but there was a traffic jam and my uber got caught in it. I wanted to be here to support my best friend and to meet the man that's captured his heart." *Wait what? Captured his heart?*

The blond man turns to me and holds out his hand. "Hi, I'm Keenan, this one's best friend."

Taking his hand, I shake it. "Everett Michaelis. His mate."

"Nice to meet you."

"Likewise."

Cotton asks, "Want to join us for lunch?"

Keenan says, "Yeah, I could eat. It'll give me a chance to pick your brains."

Cotton raises an eyebrow at him. "About what?"

Keenan grins and winks, "Whether Killua is in need of another police officer or not."

Cotton squeals and hugs Keenan. "Are you serious right now?"

Keenan laughs and tells him, "Yes, I'm serious. You know you were the only reason I stuck around the herd after my family disowned me for being gay and now that you're in Killua, well I'd rather be there too. Please don't say no because I've already arranged for movers to haul all our things to the address you gave me."

Cotton looks at me, a question in his gaze. Grinning, I kiss his temple and say to his friend, "Keenan we've got a spare room. You're welcome to use it until you find a place of your own. I've also got it on good authority that the sheriff is retiring this year and the election for his replacement will free up a deputy position."

Keenan pulls from Cotton's hug and gives me one. "Thank you!"

Chuckling, I say, "You're welcome. Any friend of Cotton's is a friend of mine. We'd be glad to have you."

Keenan points his thumb at me and tells Cotton, "This one's a keeper."

Cotton grins at me, his eyes twinkling with amusement. "He certainly is. Now, about that lunch…"

Laughing, we head out of the council building. On the walk to a restaurant, I use our mind link to ask Cotton a question.

What did Keenan mean when he said I'd captured your heart?

Exactly what he said. You've captured my heart.

Are you telling me you love me?

Cotton rolls his eyes, and says out loud, "In a roundabout way, yes. I fell hard for you over the past two weeks."

Pulling him into my arms, I plant a kiss on his lips and say with a smile on my face, "I fell hard for you too beautiful."

Keenan shouts, "Alright lovebirds, quit smooching and come on! I'm starving."

Barking out a laugh, I loop my arm through Cotton's and whisper conspiratorially, "Fates save me. He's another you."

Cotton elbows me in the ribs and chuckles. "Jerk."

"At least my life won't be boring with the two of you around."

Cotton nods sagely. "There is that."

Keenan shouts, "Come on slow pokes or I'll eat without you."

Cotton shouts back, "We're coming, you impatient overgrown child."

Keenan says, "Hey, I resent that remark," and I laugh. *Yep, life will never be boring with these two around. I can't wait to experience it.*

The End

I hope you enjoyed Everett and Cotton's story. It was a sweet fun project, and I can't wait to expand upon this world. If you haven't guessed, this story is the prequel to a brand-new series I'm planning titled Killua Mountain Bears. I don't have a set release date for book one since I hope to finish up a couple of my other series before I start it, but it is something you can expect in the future. Thank you for reading!!!

Living on the Run—H.E.A.T

Runaways—Eclipse

What About Me?—Takida

Wouldn't It Be Nice—The Beach Boys

I Can't Help Myself—Four Tops

Let Me Be Your Superhero—Smash Into Pieces

Continue reading for the blurb of one of my upcoming books titled

Love and Lethal.

Book three in the Diary of a Hitman series.

Love and Lethal

(This story is part of a series. Since this series follows the same couple, it is recommended that you read the books in order.)

Vincetti and Ever have settled into their happily ever after now that the most recent threat to their mating has been dealt with. With no new threats making themselves known, Ever plans a vacation for them both. The destination? A hotspot for couples so they can spend some alone time together.

Unbeknownst to them, just days after arrival they've landed themselves on the radar of a sinister enemy determined to test the strength of their bond with a wicked game no one has won.

Will they beat this enemy's game before time runs out? Or will they die trying?

(Warning: Contains graphic sexual content and explicit language. Not recommended for those under the age of 18.)

ACKNOWLEDGEMENTS

I want to thank my parents for supporting me no matter what I do and tolerating me when I get in the zone of writing and ignore them completely. By tolerating, I'm really saying thanks for putting up with my shit. You have no idea how much that means to me. I love you guys. I want to thank Lisa Oliver, one of my favorite authors for encouraging me to write the story speaking in my head instead of forcing myself to stick to a different stereotype and for being an amazing friend I can bounce crazy ideas off of.

I want to thank Jemma Brown for designing such amazing covers for me. I thank the readers for taking the time to read a story from an unknown author like me. I want to thank my characters for coming to me when I was at a loss as to what to write/do next. Last, of all I want to thank all the musicians out there for playing their music and inspiring me.

ABOUT THE 

Well, Ezra isn't my real name obviously, but I liked the name, so I decided to use it. I live at home with my four dogs and one cat. I started out writing hetero romance novels, but it wasn't where my heart lied. I adore all things paranormal and M/M is by far my favorite genre, so I decided to start writing Paranormal Romances. There's a guaranteed happy ending with each of my books even if it may take some time for my guys to get there. I love each and every character on the page as if they were my own children.

It sounds weird but that's how I feel about them. I've been writing for as long as I can remember but only started actively pursuing it as a career in 2014. Since I published my first book in 2014, I have written and released multiple books with many more to come. My current list of projects is longer than my arm, so I look forward to writing and creating new stories for my readers to enjoy.

OTHER BOOKS BY
Ezra Dawn

Standalones (M/F) ***No longer available**

Playboy

The Crimson Deceit

Don't Fear the Reaper

The Boy Next Door

Standalones (M/M)

Paying for Love

Law of the Irish

Practical Ghosters

Abominable What-A?

The Cursed Prince

A Raven Walks Into A Bar *Spin-Off*

The Surgeon's Instant Family *Spin-Off*

Not A Snowball's Chance in Hell

Accidental Valentine

Poke His Bear

A Silver Reckoning

Admirer's Halloween *Spin-Off*

The Warden's Easter Trap—*(You just finished it!!!)*

Asphalt Bay Pack Series (M/M)

An Alpha for the Demigod

The Enforcer's Secret Vampire

The Beta's Poison Bite

Taming the Feral Tiger

The Doctor's Demon Prince

The Leopard's Twin Troubles

The Warlock's Beautiful Bird

The Demon's Gruff Councilman

The Councilman's Miniature Companion

The Four Horsemen Collection (M/M)

The Four Horsemen

Azazel

Sen

Taz

The Graveyard Shift (M/M)

The Mortician

The Caretaker

The Director

The Florist

The Mistake *Spin-Off*

The Driver

The Ghost

Venetian Hills (M/M)

The Alpha's Master

The Second's Cursed Mate

The Beta's Second Chance

The Panther's Favorite Bully

The Demon's Mythical Birds

Risqué Business (M/M)

Be My Prince

Seeking Rayne

The Lion's Crown

Ashes of Phoenix

Paranormals of Rockydale (M/M)

Misunderstanding His Mate

The Friendly Ghost's New Beginning

Forbidden Loves (M/M)

All is Fair in Love and War

The Submission Trilogy (M/M)

The Hybrid's Submission

The Wolf's Hybrid Dom

The Hybrid's Dominant Mate

Furry Tails (M/M)

Sugar and Spice

Crimson and Clover

Watson and Sherlock

Snow and Hail

Diary of a Hitman (M/M)

Blood and Bullets

Past and Poison

Planet Xenos (M/M)

The Heir's Vampire Guardian

Boxsets (M/M)

Asphalt Bay Pack Vol. 1

The Graveyard Shift Vol. 1

Upcoming Releases:

Titles Subject to change

Death and His Necromancer—TBA

The Artist's Prickled Fancy -TBA

CONTACT THE

You can find me on Facebook, MeWe, Twitter, and on my website.

Facebook: Ezra Dawn Author or Ezra's Book Groupies

MeWe: Amanda Ezra Ezra Dawn or Ezra's Asphalt Baywatchers

Twitter: @graveshadowcrow

Website: www.ezradawnauthor.com

I look forward to hearing from you!

Want updates on my new releases, WIP's, and exclusive giveaway opportunities? Sign-up for my newsletter by following this link and filling out the form.

Newsletter: www.ezradawnauthor.com/contact